HUCKLEBERRY FINN

MARK TWAIN

www.realreads.co.uk

Retold by Anna Kirwan
Illustrated by Judith Hunt

Published by Real Reads Ltd
Stroud, Gloucestershire, UK
www.realreads.co.uk

First published in 2009
Reprinted 2011

ISBN 978-1-906230-19-7

Printed in China by Wai Man Book Binding (China) Ltd
Designed by Lucy Guenot
Typeset by Bookcraft Ltd, Stroud, Gloucestershire

CONTENTS

THE CHARACTERS

Huckleberry Finn

The river doesn't care about his name or who his friend is, but is the Mississippi carrying Huck to freedom or to hell?

Pap Finn

The most miserable low-down drunk in the county – that's the best anyone could say about Huck's daddy.

Jim

Jim believes that a man should be able to take care of his family and stand by his friends. Isn't that what freedom is for?

Mary Jane Wilks

Mary Jane has to make big decisions, and the adults aren't much help. Is a young wayfaring stranger's the best heart to trust?

The king and the duke

These two charlatans are never at a loss for a speech, but can Huck and Jim really trust them?

Aunt Sally

Tom's Aunt Sally, Aunt Polly's sister, is generous and trusting. Will she see through Huck and Tom's schemes?

Tom Sawyer

Tom thinks Huck is dead. Which of them is more surprised when they meet again? What new adventures await them?

HUCKLEBERRY FINN

If you read *Tom Sawyer*, you'll remember
Huckleberry Finn. Huck saved the Widow
Douglas' life and she gave him a home. Tom
and Huck found robbers' gold and became rich.
But Huck wasn't used to living in a house and
always wearing shoes, doing lessons, praying,
not swearing. When he couldn't stand it any
more, he escaped and felt free and satisfied.
He got a dollar a day allowance – he didn't want
more. Tom found him, though, and talked him
back into being civilised. Huck said he'd try
respectability again.

The widow's sister moved in. Miss Watson
had slaves and was forever telling Huck what
to do. She warned him about hell until Huck
wished he could be there instead of listening to
her. The widow's ideas of goodness seemed less
mean-spirited. Huck reckoned he'd go with the
widow's way – if that was possible, him being so
ignorant, ornery and low-down.

Huck's Pap had been missing more than a year. Huck didn't want to see him, 'cos he used to beat Huck. Maybe he'd drowned – but Huckleberry judged he'd turn up.

Tom invented games out of books he read, about genies, robbers, and kings. It made Huck want to learn to read. He thought Tom stretched the truth, but he did it nice as pie. Huck went to school now. He could read, write, and spell some, was up to six times seven is thirty-five. The widow said he was coming along – she wasn't ashamed of him.

But then three things happened that Huck saw meant bad luck. He accidentally killed a spider. He spilled salt, and Miss Watson kept him from throwing any over his left shoulder. Then, worst of all, he saw his Pap's footprints, with the cross on the heel, so devils wouldn't follow.

Huck ran to Judge Thatcher's, fast as he could.
'Please, take all my money,' he begged the Judge.
'I want to give it to you.'

'Is something the matter?' the Judge asked.

'Don't ask me nothing,' Huck said, 'then I
won't have to tell no lies.'

'I think I see.' Judge Thatcher knew something
was up. 'You want to sell me control of all your
property.' He wrote a contract and paid Huck
a dollar to settle it. He estimated Huck would
explain presently.

Huck sought out Jim, one of Miss Watson's slaves. Jim had children of his own, and was always friendly to Huck. Jim knew about fortune-telling and other magic. Huck asked what Pap was up to, now he was back. Jim told him, 'Yo' ole father doan' know yit what he's a-gwyne to do.' Jim saw good luck and bad competing around Huck.

Huck walked home to the widow's house. He crept into his room. There sat Pap. Huck was scared of him.

'Starchy clothes,' growled Pap. 'Think you're better'n me?'

'Maybe I ain't,' Huck said.

'I'll learn this widow to meddle! You drop that school! Puttin' on airs! Your mother couldn't read or write, none of the family couldn't. I can't! I won't stand it! Say, lemme hear you read!' Huck read about George Washington. Pap listened a minute, then knocked the book away. 'You're rich. Heard about it downriver. That's why I come. Git me that money.'

'I hain't got money, ask Judge Thatcher.'

'How about in your pocket?' Pap took Huck's only dollar and went to buy whisky.

Next day, Pap went to the Judge, but couldn't get the money. Judge Thatcher and the widow tried to get the court to declare one of them Huck's guardian, but a judge who didn't know Pap Finn said courts mustn't separate families. That pleased Pap. He told Huck he'd cowhide him black-and-blue unless he got money. Huck borrowed three dollars from Judge Thatcher. Pap took it and got drunk.

Huck didn't quit school. Pap thrashed him a few times and Huck still wouldn't give in. Pap demanded money, got drunk, got jailed, got out, thrashed Huck, demanded money. The widow told Pap to leave. Pap said he was Huck's boss, and forced Huck to live with him in an old timber cabin.

They hunted and fished, and hardly washed. Huck enjoyed that, but Pap got drunk all the time, and thrashed Huck often. Huck couldn't leave, though. Whenever Pap went to town, he locked Huck in; at night, Pap slept with the key under his head.

The widow sent a man to find Huck, but Pap's gun drove him off. Once Pap got so drunk in town, he forgot his son for three days – Huck was locked in without food. One night, Pap was so drunk he was seeing visions. He almost killed Huck with the shotgun he was aiming at his 'devils'.

Next time Pap left, Huck used an old saw-blade to cut an escape route through the logs at the cabin's far end. Pap never noticed Huck's planned escape-route.

Upcountry, snow had melted. The Mississippi's June rise began. One day, Huck found a stray canoe that had drifted downstream, and hid it. Next time Pap went to town, Huck crawled out the hole. He loaded the canoe with everything it could carry, then made it seem robbers had murdered him and thrown him in the river. Before Pap returned, Huck paddled out onto the mile-wide Mississippi – free.

Currents carried the canoe south. Huck reached Jackson's Island around dawn, and slept. When he awoke, the sun was high. He saw the ferryboat with people he knew on board – they were searching for him. He lay low, and the boat moved on.

Three days he camped there peacefully, alone. He found ripe strawberries, raspberries and grapes.

Then, on the fourth day, he found another person's campfire, and a man asleep beside it. It was Jim! Huck was so glad to see him, he called out, 'Hello, Jim!'

Jim stared. 'Doan' hurt me! I hain't done no harm to ghosts!' He'd overheard the talk that Huck had been murdered.

Huck proved he *was* alive. They made breakfast. For days, Jim had eaten only berries, and when Huck caught a big catfish they feasted. Huck told how he'd fooled Pap. Jim said it was so smart, Tom Sawyer couldn't have done better. Then Huck asked, 'How come you're here?'

Jim looked uneasy. 'You wouldn't tell on me, would you?'

'Blamed if I would.'

'I run off.'

'Jim!'

'You said you wouldn't tell!'

'I'll stick to it, honest. People can call me a low-down abolitionist – I'll never tell.'

'It 'uz dis way. Ole missus – she awluz said she wouldn't sell me down Orleans. But dey was a trader roun' lately, en I hear her tell de widder she gwyne to. She could git eight hund'd dollars for me! I never waited to hear de res'. I lit out.'

Jim had made for the river. He'd hidden on a big raft until close enough to swim to the island. He'd wanted to go all the way to Cairo,

Illinois, where the Ohio River joined the muddy
Mississippi. That was the way north. Escaped
slaves lived free, up north. Below Illinois, slave
states Kentucky, Tennessee and Arkansas lined
both Missisippi shores. 'Down the river' south
meant hellish treatment for slaves.

Huck and Jim enjoyed camping. All kinds
of things came down the swollen river. They
caught a raft. A timber house floated toward the
island. By night, they paddled out to it on the
raft. Cards and bottles lay around. Jim found a
body, which he wouldn't let Huck look at. 'He's
dead – ben shot.'

They loaded up with useful plunder, and got away. When they went through everything, they found eight dollars; also, fishing line as thick as Huck's finger, and monstrous hooks, which caught them a catfish bigger than Jim – a tasty fry!

Was anyone still searching for them? Huck disguised himself as a girl and came ashore to ask around. A lady invited 'her' in. Huck learned some folks thought Pap murdered him – they'd talked lynching, until Jim disappeared. Now some thought Jim had done it. Many wanted the reward for catching him.

17

Huck's disguise was better than his acting. The lady guessed he wasn't female. She was kind, but Huck left quickly. Bounty-hunters, she said, were searching Jackson's Island that night!

Huck and Jim loaded the raft and pushed off.
They'd tie up and sleep by daylight, so nobody'd
see Jim. They drifted eight hours a night: the
current, four miles an hour. They fished, and
swam to keep awake. It was solemn, drifting,
their talk quiet, laughter just low chuckles. Sliding
downriver that way, they passed the midnight
sparkle of St Louis.

The fifth night after that, in a bad storm, they came upon a wrecked steamboat. Huck wanted to go aboard.

'Do you reckon Tom would pass this up?' he reasoned with Jim.

They climbed aboard – and saw a light. A voice wailed, 'Please! I won't tell!'

'Y'always want more'n your share,' another said. 'You're the meanest hound in this county.' Huck spied one man tied up, two gunmen

standing over him. He heard the two decide to leave the other to sink with the wreck.

'Quick, Jim!' Huck whispered. 'Tie their boat to our raft!'

'Raf'?' Jim groaned. 'Ain' no raf' no mo' – done broke loose and gone!'

The robbers had ransacked the steamboat and loaded their skiff. In seconds, Huck and Jim were in that skiff. Cut the rope, man the oars – away!

They caught up with their raft. Huck worried about the shipwrecked men. The widow believed in pitying sinners. He and Jim dumped the plunder onto the raft, and Huck lit out. He found help to rescue them – but too late. The wreck swirled downriver, too deep in the water for survivors.

Huck got back to Jim and the raft. Nowhere else was safe and peaceful.

The haul from the wreck was prime – boots,
blankets, books. Huck read to Jim about kings
like Louis Sixteenth. Huck said royalty put on
style. He explained: everything belonged to them,
and they just sat around, except during wars.
Jim thought it foolishness, how kings behaved.

They figured they were three nights above
Cairo. They'd sell the raft and buy steamboat
passage up the Ohio, out of trouble. But the
second night, fog came on.

They couldn't run in that. Huck in the canoe towed the raft ashore to tie up, but the current tore the raft, and Jim, away. The fog was so thick now, Huck couldn't see anything.

Huck was sick afraid. He daren't paddle for fear of running into the bank. He let the river carry him. Ahead, he heard a faint whoop – Jim! They signaled that way awhile – then, no more whoops. Had Jim drowned? Then, a faraway call! They were on opposite sides of an island.

Finally, Huck found the raft again. Jim was exhausted, asleep. Huck was so relieved, he had to joke about it or feel uncomfortable. He'd tease Jim as Tom often did. His pretend awakening stretch woke Jim, who was so relieved, he hugged him. But Huck acted as if the fog, and losing one another, had all been Jim's dream, and ridiculed his joy at their reunion. Jim caught on. His dignity was offended, his feelings hurt. Then Huck was ashamed. He apologised for his trick. He hadn't known Jim would feel that way.

They talked about Cairo. Jim was excited now, close to freedom. Huck hadn't considered what he'd feel. Miss Watson would think it stealing, helping her slave escape. Huck felt low-down, stealing from someone who'd tried to help him. His conscience confused him. Jim said he'd go up north, save money, and buy his wife. Then they'd work to buy their children. If they couldn't

buy them, they'd steal them. Freedom was giving
Jim ideas. Huck worried. He couldn't decide
whether it was right or wrong to help a slave.

They saw a light – was it Cairo? Huck
paddled off to ask. Maybe he would turn Jim in.
Along came armed men in a skiff, who asked
Huck questions. They were bounty-hunters who
wanted to search Huck's raft.

'I wish you would,' Huck said. 'My folks are
on the raft, deathly ill. Please, help!' The men
feared smallpox – each of them gave Huck a
twenty-dollar gold piece to help out the 'family',
and left very quickly.

Huck's lie kept Jim safe, but soon they realised they'd missed Cairo in the fog. Now they'd have to sell the raft, and canoe back upstream.

The night got thick. They saw a steamboat heading straight at them. Jim and Huck dived overboard as the steamboat smashed through the raft. Huck dived deep, knowing a deadly thirty-foot wheel had to go over him. He stayed under about a minute and a half, then bounced up. He called Jim, over and over – no answer. Huck swam ashore.

For a few days, Huck was looked after by a family called the Grangerfords, who were involved in a murderous feud. One day Huck found himself in the midst of a gunfight, and escaped back to the river, where he found the Grangerford slaves had helped Jim repair the raft and gather supplies. 'I's mighty glad to git you back ag'in! Thought you'd ben shot.'

'Don't lose no time, Jim! Shove off for the big water!' There was no home like a raft.

More days and nights passed, quiet and lovely. The river ran a mile and a half wide. They slept days, travelled nights, dangled their legs in the water and talked.

One morning Huck found a canoe, and took it ashore to pick berries. Suddenly two men came tearing up the path, chased by other men with dogs. The two men begged for help, so Huck took them to the raft.

Huck discovered the two men were in trouble for selling tooth cleanser that dissolved teeth.

The younger said he'd been a printer, an actor, a mesmerist, and a singing geography teacher. The old bald one said he usually cured cancer or paralysis or told fortunes. The younger one sighed and said he'd fallen in fortune. He was really the exiled Duke of Bridgewater, and would like to be called 'Your Grace.' He asked Jim to wait on him.

After a while, the older one said, 'I, too, fell on hard times. I am the pore Looy the Seventeen, son of Marry Antonette! Trouble has brung these gray hairs and premature balditude.' He, too, thought he'd feel better if they served him.

Huck figured they weren't real royalty, like in books. He thought it would keep the peace, though, letting them have their way. They asked, was Jim a runaway? Huck told them Jim was his family's slave he'd inherited. He said they were travelling at night so nobody'd mistake Jim for a runaway.

Towards night, rain came. The duke and king took over the shelter and bedding, while Huck and Jim kept watch on deck. Jim watched extra hours when Huck got sleepy.

Next day, the two rogues 'laid out a campaign'
for money. From his bag, the duke produced
handbills. He said to the king, 'We'll hire a hall
and do the swordfight from Richard III and the
balcony from Romeo and Juliet. I'll learn you
Shakespeare.'

After their rehearsals, which made mincemeat
of Shakespeare, they went ashore while Jim stayed
on the raft. The little town was deserted, everyone
gone to a revival. The duke found an empty
printing shop and said he'd stay there
while the king and Huck went to
the camp-meeting to fleece the
faithful. The king could really
preach. He told the people he
used to be a pirate, but was
saved and was now a
missionary. He took
up a collection.

The duke, meanwhile, used the print shop as if he owned it. By the time they got back to the river, the pair had made $97.25. The duke had posters for their show, and had made an advertisement for a runaway slave, reward offered. It described Jim! The duke said they could travel by daylight now. If anyone came near, they'd tie Jim, and say they were after the $200 bounty. They all thought that would work.

The next few days, the royalty rehearsed. They jumped around, whacked each other with wooden swords, and shouted speeches. One morning in Arkansas, they hid the raft, and went to find a place to perform.

Luckily, a circus was in Brickville, and people already arriving for the show. The duke hired the court-house and hung posters. Considerable drinking was going on, and things got rowdy. Only a few people came to see 'Shakespeare.' Next morning, the duke said what the people wanted was low comedy.

He painted a sign for a play called 'The Royal Nonesuch.' It said, 'Ladies and Children Not Admitted.'

That night, the audience was packed with men expecting something special. The curtain went up. The king pranced out on all fours, naked, painted all colours! Everyone roared with laughter. Two minutes later, the curtain came down. The duke sauntered out and said 'the tragedy' would be performed for two more nights, so they should tell their friends. Everyone who'd paid thought he'd been cheated.

The next night,
after selling the
last ticket, the duke
pulled Huck out the
back door. These
customers weren't
newcomers. They
were last night's
audience, who had
returned with rotten
vegetables and
eggs to pelt the old
frauds.

Safe, heading
downriver, they
laughed. They'd taken that town for $465.

That night, Jim said, 'Dey's reg'lar rapscallions,
Huck.'

'Kings is kings,' Huck figured. 'They're an
ornery lot. It's how they're raised. You got to
make allowances.'

Huck slept, while Jim stood watch. When Huck awoke at daybreak, Jim was mourning to himself. Huck knew he was missing his wife and children. He expected never to see them again. Huck saw that Jim loved them deeply, and it troubled him.

That day, they heard news. A man called Mr Peter Wilks had just died, leaving his estate to three nieces and his two brothers, who were expected to arrive soon from England.

This interested the king, and he listened out for details. When he and the duke talked it over, they decided to leave Jim on the raft and pose as the Wilks brothers from England, coming to help and grieve with their nieces, Mary Jane, Susan and Joanna. The king's accent was terrible. The duke supposedly couldn't hear or speak. Huck was their valet.

Most people in town hadn't met any foreigners. The Wilks girls didn't know their English uncles, but were ready to love them dutifully. A friend, the doctor, advised caution, but they welcomed the imposter 'uncles' who leaned over the coffin, weeping piteously. Peter Wilks' will left them all something: houses, a tannery, some slaves, and $6000.

Mary Jane invited them to stay at the house. By nightfall, the royal 'uncles' had their hands on the money. The king hid the $6000 in his mattress, but he wasn't done scheming. Huck wanted to warn Mary Jane, but if he exposed the thieves what would happen to him and to Jim?

Next morning, the girls asked about England. Huck got everything wrong. Mary Jane wouldn't let her sisters doubt his word, though. Huck appreciated her kindness. He couldn't let these girls be robbed! 'Uncle Harvey' wanted to sell everything after the funeral, and told the nieces they'd live with him in England. Huck saw he had to rescue that money from the mattress. He would swipe it, hide it, and when he and Jim got away, he'd write Mary Jane and tell where it was.

It wasn't hard to snitch the money bag, but Huck had to hide it well. Late that night, he crept downstairs, but the front door was locked.

Someone was coming! He ducked into the parlour, where the corpse lay until burial. Hearing steps approaching closer, Huck thrust the money-bag deep into the coffin, and hid behind the door. Mary Jane came in to weep and pray. Huck didn't want to leave the money there, but he had to. He got back upstairs unseen, but worried.

The funeral was next day, and the money was buried along with Uncle Peter. The king arranged to auction off the Wilks property that very week. Before the girls realised what was happening, the slaves they knew and loved had been sold down the river, mother and children separated. Mary Jane and her sisters were shocked and miserable.

The king and duke learned the money-bag was gone. They grilled Huck. Had he been in there? Huck said he'd seen slaves tiptoe out – the same ones who'd now been sold. That fixed the old humbugs!

Later, though, he came upon Mary Jane, crying. She was so beautiful and kind, Huck couldn't bear it. He knew, once the 'uncles'' deception was revealed, everything they'd sold would be recovered. He had to comfort her. 'Your slaves will be back, and together, I know it!'

Mary Jane hugged him. 'Say it again!' she begged.

Huck reckoned, in a tight place, telling the truth
was risky. He lacked experience at it. But, 'I got to
tell the truth,' he explained. 'Brace up, it's bad. These
uncles are frauds.' He told her everything. Her eyes
blazed. Huck promised he could stop them, but he
had to do it his way, to protect someone else. She said
she'd do whatever he needed. He told her to keep
away all day – her face would show she knew. That
night, she could get the scoundrels jailed. If he got
caught with them, she'd vouch for him. If he was

gone, she could inquire at Brickville about the Royal Nonesuch for more proof they were fakes.

He couldn't bring himself to tell her where the money was. He was glad he had enough schooling to write an explanation that Mary Jane could read later.

Mary Jane thanked him fervently, took his hand, and said she'd pray for him. Huck thought, if she knew him better, she'd take on a job more her size. If he'd thought it would do any good, he'd have prayed for her, she was so sweet.

The houses were auctioned that afternoon. During the sale, a steamboat landed, bringing Peter Wilks' friends: his doctor, his lawyer, and a man who declared he'd seen the king and Huck in town before they claimed they'd arrived. Could they prove their identity?

The king said their baggage and identification hadn't arrived yet. 'Uncle Harvey's' accent didn't convince those few who'd travelled, and the newcomers laughed at the idea of Huck being English. 'Reckon you ain't used to lying,' the lawyer told him. 'You do it pretty awkward.' Then he tried a trick. He asked the king to describe Peter's tattoo.

'A thin blue arrow,' the king announced, 'hard to see.' The undertaker hadn't noticed any tattoo.

The crowd made their feelings known. 'They're frauds! Ride 'em on a rail!'

'Gentlemen!' the lawyer said. 'There's one way to know. Dig up the coffin.'

The crowd made it clear – if no tattoo existed, they'd lynch them, Huck included! They surged toward the graveyard. It was the worst danger

Huck had ever been in. A storm was coming on, and it was getting dark. If only the man guarding him'd get distracted, it'd be a good time to leave.

Lit by flickering lightning, they dug up the coffin, lifted the lid. Everyone crowded forward. Somebody shouted, 'Here's the bag of gold!'

Huck's captor dropped his grip in the excitement. Huck lit out, back through the empty town. A light burned in Mary Jane's window! His heart swelled, but he had to get to the raft.

When he reached the river, he found a canoe and struck out full-steam. He fell onto the raft alongside Jim, exhausted. 'Set her loose, Jim! Glory be, we're shut of them!'

They took off. But, next lightning flash, they saw a skiff following. The royalty!

The king grabbed Huck, shook him, and said, 'Tired of our company?'

'No, your majesty,' Huck said. 'When they found the gold, the man holding me let go. I lit out.'

'Leggo the boy,' the duke said. 'Did *you* inquire

around for him when *you* got loose?' The two of them suspected each other of hiding the swag, intending to come back alone to retrieve it. They bickered until the duke started choking the king, who had to give in. Then they started scheming again. Jim and Huck worried. What was next? Housebreaking? Counterfeiting?

They were far south now. The frauds reckoned they were out of danger, but none of the angles they'd played before made money. One morning, the king went ashore to see if anyone there had heard of the Nonesuch. By the time the duke and Huck found him, he was drunk. While the two royals argued, Huck slipped away, back to Jim and the raft.

But Jim was gone. Huck saw a boy nearby, and asked if he'd seen anyone by Jim's description. 'Yes,' the boy said, 'he's a runaway. They've got him at Phelps' sawmill. $200 reward! Old fellow who nailed him had to go upriver and couldn't wait to collect, so he sold his rights for $40!

Huck asked what the 'old fellow' had looked like. It was the king! After all that journey, everything Jim and Huck had done for those scoundrels, they did that to Jim, made him a slave again for life for $40.

Huck felt low. Maybe providence was slapping him for his wickedness. Huck tried to promise heaven he'd write to Miss Watson so she could claim her legal rights to Jim. But he couldn't do it. He found out, you can't pray a lie. He thought over the trip downriver with Jim – he couldn't harden his heart. He remembered every time Jim stood watch for him, and how glad Jim was when he got back safe after they got separated. Jim hugged him and called him 'honey' the way he did his own children. After the lie to the bounty-hunters, Jim had called Huck his best friend – his only friend.

Huck knew he had to decide whose side to be on. He studied a minute, then said to himself,

All right then, I'll go to hell. He'd steal Jim out of slavery again.

He hid the raft, put on his best clothes, then paddled the canoe to Phelps' sawmill where Jim was being held. He hid the canoe and headed for the house. Hounds in the yard barked, then a woman appeared. 'It's you, at last! Children!' she called, hugging him and drawing him indoors. 'It's your cousin Tom!' Then, to Huck, 'Uncle Silas went to fetch you. Wasn't he at the landing?'

'No, ma'am.'

'Not "ma'am" – Aunt Sally,' she chided.

'How's Sis? How's everybody?'

Huck was up a stump. Just in time, Aunt Sally grabbed him and hid him behind the bed. 'Here he comes! We'll play a joke!' Huck was in a sweat.

'Hasn't he come?' Aunt Sally asked the old gentleman when he came in. 'Goodness, where can he be?' She carried on like that, then said, 'Why, look yonder!' When her husband peered out the window, Aunt Sally produced her surprise.

'Who's that?' Uncle Silas cried.

'It's Tom Sawyer!' she announced, pleased as pie.

Huck almost collapsed with surprise and relief. He felt reborn. They asked about Sid, Mary and Aunt Polly. Being Tom was easy and comfortable – until he heard a steamboat coming downriver. What if Tom arrived and shouted

Huck's name? Huck said he had to go get his baggage, and took the horse and wagon.

Halfway to town, here came a wagon carrying Tom! Tom gasped and said, 'I hain't ever done you no harm – why'd you want to come back to ha'nt me?'

'I hain't come back,' Huck said. 'I hain't been gone.'

'Warn't you murdered?'

'No, I played it. You come feel of me if you don't believe me.' Tom was mighty glad. Huck told him the fix he was in, and asked what Tom reckoned they'd better do. Tom devised a plan. Huck would take Tom's trunk back as his baggage. Tom would come a bit later. At first, Huck shouldn't let on he knew him.

Then Huck told him there was another problem – Miss Watson's Jim was the Phelps' captive, and Huck was trying to steal him out of slavery.

'But, Jim is ... ' Tom stopped and thought. Huck felt low-down.

'I know it's dirty business,' he told Tom, 'but I'm a-going to free him, and I want you to keep mum.'

'I'll help you,' Tom said. Huck was astonished, but Tom started planning. He'd show up at the Phelps' place at dinnertime, pretending he was his half-brother, Sid.

The plan worked. Over dinner, Huck and Tom listened for news of Jim. Finally, the little boys asked to go to 'the show'. Uncle Silas said there wouldn't be one – the runaway they'd captured had told him about that scandalous show. Nobody was going.

Huck and Tom retired early, then climbed out the window, intending to warn the duke and king they'd been rumbled. In town, they met a noisy rush of people with torches. The crowd had the duke and the king, tarred and feathered. They were riding them out of town on a sharp split rail. It was so cruel, Huck felt sorry. He thought he'd never feel any hardness toward the old fools again.

They returned to the sawmill.

'I bet I know where Jim is,' Tom said. 'That hut. They take vittles back there and unlock it. It's Jim!'

What brains Tom had, Huck thought. He'd tried to plan how to free Jim, but he knew Tom would invent something better. Still, he didn't understand why a respectable character like Tom would stoop to stealing a slave. Yet Tom was absolutely for it.

Next day, they went down to the hut. There was one window-hole. 'Simple,' Huck said.

'Too simple,' Tom decided.

'We could saw him out like I done before I was murdered,' Huck suggested.

'That's more like! Mysterious, troublesome – good! But we can do more. Ain't no hurry.' They pried open the lean-to behind the hut. There was no door in to Jim, but there were shovels and a dirt floor: they could dig Jim out. It would take longer than sawing or the window, but Tom explained there was more honour, accomplishing tasks despite dangerous difficulties.

Tom talked to the black field-hand bringing Jim's food. He let them visit Jim, who was overjoyed.

'Don't let on you know us,' Tom whispered. 'If you hear digging, it's us. We're setting you free.' Jim only had time to clasp Tom's hand before they had to go.

Tom invented a sure-fire complicated escape. He thought of everything. Jim was chained by one leg to his bedstead. Lifting the bed would free him if he carried the chain, but Tom thought sawing the bed's leg would be better. Instead of lanterns, they'd gather rotten fox-fire bark for light. Tom could complicate anything until it was elegant.

Tom and Huck helped Jim scratch messages here and there. They stole sheets to make a rag rope, and got it to him baked inside a pie.

They were all proud of that.

Huck was getting nervous. Aunt Sally had sent news to Louisiana about Jim. Soon Miss Watson and the Widow Douglas would know where he was.

But Tom said they weren't finished making it a first-class escape. They did everything the best books recommended. Jim appreciated their resolve to do it right. Finally, after about three weeks, they were ready for the last detail. Tom said there had to be a 'nonnomous' warning. He wrote: 'Beware. Trouble brewing. Cut-throat gang will steal your runaway tonight.' Huck slipped it under the Phelps' door. He didn't realise the reaction it'd get.

After dinner, Aunt Sally knew Huck was up to something. She sent him into the parlour to wait for her. There were fifteen farmers in there, with guns! They meant to stop the gang from stealing Jim! Huck was anxious to get away and warn Tom. As soon as Aunt Sally sent him upstairs, he climbed out and ran for the hut.

Tom was thrilled. They heard the men
coming as they squeezed out through the lean-
to. They got to the fence, and Jim and Huck got
over, but Tom's britches caught.

Bang! Bang! Bullets whizzed past. 'After
'em! Turn loose the dogs!' The dogs knew
them, though, and ran past. The escapees
got to the waterside where Huck had left the
canoe. They headed for the island, and at last,
fell onto the raft.

'Now, Jim, you're a free man again,' Huck said. 'I bet you won't ever be a slave no more.'

'It 'uz planned beautiful en it 'uz done beautiful!' Jim rejoiced. They were all glad, especially Tom, because he'd been shot in the leg. He was bleeding. Huck and Jim consulted.

'If't was him being sot free en some'un got shot, would Tom Sawyer say, "Nemmine 'bout a doctor?"' Jim said. 'Well, den, I doan budge 'til de doctor lookit dat laig.'

Tom raised a fuss, but Huck went.

He told the doctor his brother got hurt hunting; they'd rather their folks didn't know. The doctor agreed to go, but he didn't trust the canoe to carry two. Huck told him where to find Tom, then started back to the Phelps' house.

He met Uncle Silas, told him he and Sid had followed the men last night, but got separated. He said Sid had just gone to town for news of the gang.

Next morning, the doctor arrived with men carrying a sick, feverish Tom. They had Jim, too. Some folks talked of hanging him to set an example. Others said he was valuable – his owner would pay for him. The doctor came out and said, 'Treat him well. He could've run, but he saved that boy instead.' They stopped cussing Jim, but they did lock him up.

It was another day before Tom woke in his right mind. 'Where's the raft? Where's Jim? Did you tell Aunty the story, how we set him free?' Aunt Sally thought he was raving, but Tom decided to tell her the full story of Jim's escape.

'So it was you little rapscallions!' she scolded. 'No more meddling with that runaway!'

Tom rose up in bed. 'Turn him loose! He ain't no slave! Miss Watson died two months ago. She was ashamed she thought of selling him – she set him free in her will!' His eyes widened then. 'Aunt Polly!'

Tom's Aunt Polly was standing right there. 'Didn't you get my letter?' she asked as Aunt Sally hugged her. 'You wrote me about 'Sid,' and Sid's at home – What are *you* doing here, Huckleberry Finn?'

So another deception was uncovered. Aunt Polly confirmed what Tom had said about Miss Watson's will. Tom had plotted to free Jim, knowing he'd never be a slave again. The opportunity had been just too good to miss.

Huck brought Jim up to Tom's room to talk. When the adults heard how he'd helped the doctor, everyone made a fuss over Jim. Tom suggested to Huck that they and Jim go out west among the Indians. Huck said it would suit him, but he couldn't afford to buy an outfit. He reckoned by now Pap had got his money from Judge Thatcher and drunk it up.

'No, he hain't,' Tom said. 'Money's all there.'

'Yo' Pap ain't a-comin' back no mo',' Jim said. ''Member dat house wuz float'n, en dey wuz a dead man? Dat wuz him.'

So, Huck thought maybe he'd light out for Indian Territory. Aunt Sally was starting to talk about adopting and civilising him. He couldn't stand for that. He'd been there before.

TAKING THINGS FURTHER

The real read

This *Real Read* version of *Huckleberry Finn* is a retelling of Mark Twain's magnificent work. If you would like to read the full novel in all its original splendour, many complete editions are available, from bargain paperbacks to beautifully bound hardbacks. You will be able to find a copy in your local library or bookshop.

Filling in the spaces

The loss of so many of Mark Twain's original words is a sad but necessary part of the shortening process. We have had to make some difficult decisions, omitting subplots and details, some important, some less so, but all interesting. We have also, at times, taken the liberty of combining two events into one, or of giving a character words or actions that originally belong to another. The points below will fill in some of the gaps, but nothing can beat the original.

- The original *Huckleberry Finn* is told entirely in the first person by Huck.

- By writing about Jim's supposed magical powers of fortune-telling, Twain shows how much faith people, including Huck, place in his spiritual and ritual knowledge.

- Jim speaks in a distinct dialect, evident in this *Real Read* version of *Huckleberry Finn*. In the original, Twain claims to have portrayed seven different Mississippi River dialects.

- Huck kills a rattlesnake and leaves it on Jim's blanket as a prank. It attracts a live snake, which bites Jim. He develops a fever, and is in danger for four days and nights.

- When Huck disguises himself as a girl, his visit to Mrs Loftus makes a funny, subtle story commenting on gender expression.

- The original contains vivid descriptions of flooded woodlands, lightning storms, white water currents taking control of raft and canoe, and the river's abundant wildlife.

- While Huck is the guest of the Grangerford family, he witnesses his friend Buck's attempt to shoot a neighbour. When Huck inadvertently helps Buck's sister to elope, the feud erupts into active warfare. Huck watches in horror as Buck and his cousin are killed. He later learns that the eloping lovers have escaped safely.

- When the king and duke are trying to swindle the Wilks girls, Mark Twain includes many more layers of trickery. The real uncles arrive from England, and are met with suspicion. The king and duke end up losing all the money they had made earlier to the Wilks girls.

- Tom's escape plan for Jim, as contrived by Mark Twain, is much more elaborate than in this version.

Back in time

Mark Twain is the pen-name of Samuel Langhorne Clemens (1835–1910), Southerner turned Westerner turned Easterner turned European resident and world traveller – and back again; he ended his days in Connecticut. During his varied life, Twain was a newspaper correspondent, a steamboat pilot, a mineral prospector, a stage humourist, and for many years America's best-known writer. He chose his pen-name because 'mark twain!' was the call of the leadsman when a great steam paddle-wheeler was in water two fathoms deep, just enough to be safe.

Twain's most famous creations, *Tom Sawyer* and *Huckleberry Finn*, have become two of the world's great literary archetypes of boyhood. The books are often required reading in schools, in spite of claims that they are subversive and encourage bad behaviour.

Huckleberry Finn, published in 1884, is set in little river towns along the Mississippi River, sometime in the 1850s, after the Mexican War and before the Civil War, and thus before President Abraham Lincoln's Emancipation Proclamation freed America's slaves. Missouri was a southern, slave-holding state, and it bordered the western frontier, where native tribal life was being over-run by white settlers.

In a slave-labour economy, some people are treated as chattels, 'animals' that belong to their 'owners' and can be bought and sold, rather than citizens with personal rights. Mark Twain believed that slavery not only oppressed its victims, but also corrupted the mental freedom of the slave-owners. From the outset, Huck and Tom have enough money to buy Jim outright and free him, but it never occurs to any of them that such a simple choice is available. They have not been taught to think that way.

Mark Twain identified, once and for all, one of the most pain-inflicting obscenities that can legally be pronounced in English – nigger, 'the n-word'. By putting it so relentlessly on the lips of his most ignorant characters, Twain intentionally showed how language itself can so easily support both conscious and unaware bigotry.

Finding out more

We recommend the following resources:

Books

- Susan Bivin Aller, *Mark Twain* (Just The Facts Biographies), Lerner, 2006.

- April Jones Prince, *Who Was Mark Twain?*, Grosset and Dunlap, 2004.

- R. Kent Rasmussen, *Mark Twain for Kids: His Life and Times*, Chicago Review Press, 2004.

Websites

- www.cmgww.com/historic/twain
The official website of Mark Twain's estate.

- www.marktwainhouse.org
The Victorian mansion of the Clemens family in Hartford, Connecticut, is a fascinating museum of the author's life and era.

- www.mohistory.org
The Missouri Historical Society – search here for 'Mark Twain'.

- www.nationalgeographic.com/railroad/tl
Timeline of the history of slavery in America.

- www.waymarking.com
Search for 'Underground Railroad' for a list of historical sites connected with the secret escape routes and safe houses used by abolitionists to assist the liberated refugees.

Films

- *The Adventures of Huckleberry Finn*, starring Mickey Rooney and Rex Ingram, directed by Richard Thorpe, MGM, 1939. Closer to the text than many Hollywood treatments.

- *The Adventures of Huckleberry Finn*, starring Eddie Hodges and Archie Moore, directed by Michael Curtiz, MGM, 1960.

- *Huckleberry Finn*, starring Ron Howard, Donny Most and Antonio Fargas, directed by Robert J. Totten, Starz/Anchor Bay, 1975.

- *The Adventures of Huckleberry Finn*, starring Elijah Wood and Courtney Vance, directed by Stephen Sommers, Walt Disney Pictures, 1993.

- *Mark Twain*, directed by Ken Burns, Florentine Films, 2001.

Music

- *Big River*, MCA Records. The Tony-award winning Roger Miller musical.

Food for thought

Here are some things to think about if you are reading *Huckleberry Finn* alone, or ideas for discussion if you are reading it with friends.

In retelling *Huckleberry Finn* we have tried to recreate, as accurately as possible, Mark Twain's original plot and characters. We have also tried to imitate aspects of his style. Remember, however, that this is not the original work; thinking about the points below, therefore, can help you begin to understand Mark Twain's craft. To move forward from here, turn to the full-length version, called *The Adventures of Huckleberry Finn*, and lose yourself in his wonderful story telling.

Starting points

• How do you feel about Huck? Do your feelings change as you read his adventures?

• How do you think Jim felt about Miss Watson? And about Huck and Tom?

- How do Huck's feelings about Jim develop during the adventure?

- Do you think Huck makes mistakes? If so, what do you think he learns from them?

Themes

What do you think Mark Twain is saying about the following themes in *Huckleberry Finn*?

- truth and lies
- freedom
- loyalty
- superstition

Style

Can you find paragraphs containing examples of the following?

- descriptions of setting and atmosphere
- the use of humour

- different characters speaking in distinctive ways

- the use of imagery to enhance description

Look closely at how these paragraphs are written. What do you notice? Can you write a paragraph in the same style?

Symbols

Writers frequently use symbols in their work to deepen the reader's emotions and understanding. Mark Twain is no exception. Think about how the symbols in this list match the action in *Huckleberry Finn*.

- the river

- islands

- the raft

- clothing and shoes

- money